BOOKS BY SAM HAMILL

Poetry
Heroes of the Teton Mythos
Petroglyphs
The Calling Across Forever
The Book of Elegiac Geography
Triada
animae
Requiem
Fatal Pleasure

Essays
At Home in the World

Translation
The Lotus Lovers
(*poems by Tzu Yeh and Li Ch'ing-chao*)
Night Traveling
(*lyrics from classical Chinese*)
The Same Sea in All of Us
(*Selected poems of Jaan Kaplinski*)

FATAL PLEASURE

FATAL PLEASURE

Sam Hamill

Breitenbush Books
Portland, Oregon

Library of Congress Cataloging in Publication Data

Hamill, Sam.
    Fatal pleasure.

    I. Title.
PS3558.A4235F3   1984   811'.54   83-15488
ISBN (cloth) 0-932576-18-4
ISBN (paper) 0-932576-19-2

Breitenbush Books are published for James Anderson by:
Breitenbush Publications
P.O. Box 02137
Portland, Oregon 97202

The author would like to thank the National Endowment for the Arts for a Writing Fellowship in 1981 during which time many of these poems were written. Thanks to PEN American for an emergency grant during a time of crises. And thanks to Robert Hass for his encouragement and critical assistance.

C. P. Cavafy's "He Swears" is reprinted from *Collected Poems*, translated by Edmund Keeley and Philip Sherrard, by permission of Princeton University Press and Mr. Keeley.

Thanks to the following who first published many of these poems:

Columbia: "Nihil Obstat" and "October Frost"
Copper Canyon Press: "Requiem" and "The Cartographer's Wedding"
Mississippi Mud: "Anybody's Genius" and "The Journey"
Memphis State Review: "Homage To Trakl"
The Port Townsend Leader: "In Gemini"
Catalyst: "The Body of Summer" and "After Bilitis"
Bumbershoot: "Vespers"
Alaska Quarterly Review: "A Rose for Solitude"
Hanging Loose: "In the Company of Men" and "Loyalty"
Dalmo'ma: "Kah Tai Purgatorio"
Yakima and Blue Begonia Press: "The Oracle at Sunrise"

CONTENTS

FATAL PLEASURE

to Kuan Yin

HE SWEARS

He swears every now and then to begin a better life.
But when night comes with its own counsel,
its own compromises and prospects—
when night comes with its own power
of a body that needs and demands,
he returns, lost, to the same fatal pleasure.

C. P. Cavafy

OCTOBER FROST

THE POOR CRICKET longs for a song, and I
know it, I can feel it in the air
at dusk when shadows swirl and October frost
settles all the dust.
           Between us on this table,
a bottle of warm red wine, the pen,
the ashtray, and the wood. Soon enough,
the dark will nail us down. Our hands
hold a cup, a knife, a noose.
           Even for a cricket,
song may mean no more than an act
of contrition, unreasonable fear of the dark,
or its own expression of this alien life
on a fertile, fading planet.
           Whatever
we lose or have lost, we find it
elsewhere, in someone else's hands, and we know
that something's wrong that has no name
of its own.
        The poor, poor cricket
wants to sing. The dust begins to freeze.
In some other country, in some other time,
he might mean something, he might be important
enough to cage.
        But it is the end of the day
at the end of October when the year begins
to close. In the wine cup, in the pen or the air,
we can feel it in our bones: we don't belong.

The poor poet wants a dithyramb.
The cricket longs for a song.

REQUIEM

for Kenneth Rexroth 1905-1982

> *Here too we find virtue somehow rewarded,*
> *Tears in the nature of things, hearts touched by human transience.*
> *—Virgil*

REQUIEM

ALL DAY I wandered the difficult reverie of the sea
and the sea sang back to me that old song
of summer, "To Love is to Live," and the sun settled
lightly in the sea. The interstellar silence between rainfall
and rainfall is all
that we need know of love, and all that we may learn of life
is that to die need not mean death.

The old hull that slowly disintegrates among the stones
of its long last resting place bears a silence
heavy like a shadow; the iron railings flaking
off into rust, the old battered timbers nourishing salt air
and sea mist. But there was a time it
creaked with delight and bore tuna in its hold and strong
young men worked its shifting decks.

Now that the nets are gone, the brass fittings stripped from the
wheelhouse, cobwebbed and dark, now that the anchor
is dragged away? The tedious afternoons that pass us by
unnoticed are the epics of our days. The tides
do not respect our work. And yet, to work
is the meaning of the tides as they slowly eat away
the memories of old labors we abandon.

Because it is summer and the sea is beautiful, we think it
enough just to be here, walking, sighing
to the sighs of the sea. There were others
who walked this beach to sing
a little song of charity and death. They still sing, but far beyond
our ears. Few are they who hold in mind our prehistoric life.
Fewer still will learn to bow to what they cannot have.

Even in dry summer the sea winds sing our praise. But we
think it a cold song, shudder, and complain and turn away.
Farther from home than we ever thought we could be,
the days break over us like dreams the rains
can't wash away. If *to live* means *to love*,
to work gives form to what we say: each day
we struggle to make the day.

There was a man, now gone, who sang this song to me.
I didn't believe it then. He begged a price
I didn't know how to pay. But now that he is gone,
dead as they say, I place my trust in him, in eighty years
of faith, his long life's love that settles down
like rain into the sea, lightly down on everything,
like breath settles lightly into air.

SUPPOSE ONE human voice must speak,
suppose one human sound must stretch
across the numberless gray casts of evening, in chill
of hoarfrost before the puffs of hope
chimneys breathe against despair—then let
that voice be calming, a warming sound that bends
against the air curving back
across the breath it comes from, that no one hear
without the deliberate act of listening. Our time
is near. The animal-like phrases
we attempt to trap in voices
move beyond our eyes, shadows
melting into shadows
we never learned to read.

When a man ascends the stage of his own imagining,
he delivers there the grand summation
of his suffering, his one long
accounting of this days that disappeared
more quickly than his faith. His song
is plain. His music
lowly, like his shame. The stillness in the air
at eventide, the stillness in the leaves at that
singular moment before they ride
the last ride down to earth, the still perfectly still
body of the hunter with his finger on the trigger
squeezing lightly between the hammers of his heart—
these motionless moments
we only glimpse in passing.

And after love, after the cry of love
is stoppered in the throat, these little revolutions
of the soul are caught between the breath
and the breath, between the blood
and the body in its tremors. Who then
will remember the ambiguity of desire, the duplicity

hidden in the semi-public kiss? Per-
functory and self-serving. Wavering,
hesitant, faulty, . . . no wonder
we strangle on these doubts. Raccoons that haunt
these shores blend into the dusk. Can we
do less? We see them
walk on tiny hands to steal the scraps we leave.

It is only when we must move, similarly simply,
toward that secret something
basic as our breathing that we
can learn to trust. What troubles us
most deeply is ourselves—a voice that longs to make
itself into a fist or hand
to touch. We want to slow our pace
to match the little steps of animals that feed at night.
If we must blend into the blending grays
of dusk, then we must
learn to wait, watching from the corners of our eyes
until the remembered glimpse of warming fires
blazes up again
a long way down that coast around the bend
where evening fog comes toward us hushed and slowly
like a friend.

Out the long road with its ruts and cracks
and tire-battering patches, past fields
of spotted cows and fatted summer horses, past
the few last stands of woods, past new houses
with indoor plumbing and interest rates,
out,
past the end of the city water line and up
the hill beyond the old shake mill into
a world of promise,

and then down the dirt county road
lined with alder and evergreen, broadleaf
fern, rhododendron, camas,
and camomile, and up
the narrow drive where
branches batter my battered truck,

I wheeze
to a stop. The brief northwestern summer allows
a little dust
to remind me
of all those summers back

in that country I'll never shake
from my boots: the red dust
and prickly heat. Now scraggle of underbrush
almost too thick to walk through,
but I walk out
climbing through it, smelling it,
watching for juncos and thrushes and swallows,
my boots growing damp from night-mist,
my senses

confused with the memory: Wasatch,
Rockies, Tetons, Sangre de Cristos, Chugach,
and suddenly

the Olympics, ten years ago, immensely blue
in the distance. And I remember
how the rain never stops in Ketchikan,
how the rain never came
to Utah,
        all those difficult countries now
one country in
my mind . . . so different, so lonely
that poetry can't reach it; nor can I.

But I wade through it, tangle
and bramble, I wade and I plunge
through rotting broken limbs and twigs toward
bluffs rising over the Sound where winds
grow thick with the salt-smells
and islands in the distance
rise, rise and fall
in the swells: San Juans, Queen Charlottes
of Canada; and beyond them, across the long
Pacific Rim, Japan
and northern China. I would speak
across the years. T'ao Ch'ien, do
you hear?
        And why is it
I must come out here alone? Never with
a friend. For a man, for a man
in the middle of his years, there is a need
without name, an old memory or promise
broken: my mother, almost eighty now, but years
and years ago, my mother, her eyes a river
of tears for something I'd done
for no reason.

Gull-cries.
Cormorant scuds.

Clouds and clouds and clouds.
My father four years dead
and buried in that half-imagined land
of twenty-five years of fable. He died
holding a good woman's hand. I learn to live
alone
in a house I slowly build and know
my daughter likewise
will wound me. My brown Persephone so far away,
listen to this sea!

It churns, it breaks against the black
basaltic bluffs, and in the blue
swirl and curl of water, the tentacles
of kelp beds absently waver.

Suppose I cried out against
the immensity of these blues—*ocean, sky,*
or *mountain*? Would anyone hear or care? I wouldn't
give a damn if they did. When the sun
begins its fall, it makes me
sickly dizzy—birds, suns, and sea-wrack. I'd paint
these mountains black. Little wonder
old Jeffers grew so vile: he knew
what he felt inside.

Thirty years ago I used to lie
on my back in the haystack to listen to the stars.
Dusk then
was a kind of silence I haven't heard since, the unutterable
gray dying out of light across a range of gutted
mountains smoky-black with greed.

So lie quiet.

Listen. Is that
the first nighthawk searching
yellow evening light? The sound
of evening appetites:
peee-ik   peee-ik   peee-ik.

Turning to the trail back home, there is
so much vanishing behind us, so very much
to come, and all that country,
spread out beyond all comprehension,
beyond imagination.
Pray that it will heal.

Coming across me here, along these old
logging trails, along these game trails leading us
back from the sea, do you think
me a gentle man, but sad? —not unlike
that man you knew once as a child,
who wagered with the sun
and lost,
who made you lovely promises—so long ago
that you can't seem to remember,

although you remembered
for a time. This sea, you think,
smells like the great salt wastelands of
the west. The same gulls break and cry. The same hearts
break night after night
when the same voices
steal into our sleep. Kochininako, Yellow Woman,
take my hand. This silence
that steals into my speech is there because there are
so many promises
I've tried and tried to keep.

Is IT STILL there, Canyon de Chelly,
its high walls streaked
the color of new blood or of fire?

Once, a long time ago it is true, but once
I went there alone, looking
for god-knows-what and found what the Greeks
called *Eikos*, a holy place,

and the evening sunlight there was orange,
fiery as all history, and I walked for a time
in no particular direction, lost
for all purpose, but
learning,
slowly learning: apple trees, pear trees,
a spotted pony in a narrow corral.

I was a child of no country
but the country of the heart. I felt
the hands of the dead slide up
beneath my shirt. And now when I write or speak
there is dying in my hands, dying
to flavor my speech.

I tried to sleep. A quarter moon
slipped over the canyon rim to filter
through the trees. The flanks of the canyon
were fleshy in a light
as after twilight
when I rose from a brown saddle blanket
to walk among the shades; my body
moved as though it belonged
to another, the old melancholy
dragging me down into the past.

But every canyon, like every street,
is a doorway, and we are beggars
softly knocking for entry. The busy people
pass us by in silence, their eyes focused carefully
an inch beyond our heads or
just beyond our feet. For fear,
they look away. Our secret whispered entreaties
are fruitless, falling
like dry leaves through summer drought,
and we turn again
toward night and thirst of heat.

Did I sleep? I remembered the body
of a woman I loved once who
wouldn't speak, how, with her child
nursing, her breasts dried up, and nothing, she said,
would ever be the same. Her furtive eyes
glistened in the dark like little fires
burning on a hill, and I held her face
for nothing in my hands until
I thought it would break.

The sweet, delicious smell
of rain.

So many years
since the hoeing. It is too easy
saying, Here is Ira Hayes
dying in a ditch. My people were not heroes, but died
there too. No one mourned their passing
except when the crop was good.

The waters and the beggars
come and go, the cruel light of years
claws across our eyes. Are there still
memories in the ashes

rains wash slowly from the canyon? The memory
of women weaving baskets
from a time before they were meant for tourists? Is anguish
the only sound of water? Or is it
longing. And what would it mean
if we could walk again together
through ruins the years have left behind, our hands
together,
our eyes steady on
each other's eyes, and in our hearts
the flicker of a song? Would the same crickets
sing down there along the river
if we paused for love on the bank?

I who inhabit
the river-with-one-bank
have been too long with the sea, too long with
the slow rub of fog
and all those old songs
of the dying.
              Now, when light rain comes calling,
when it kisses the edge of my sleep, I dream
of scarlet ocotillo flowers
blooming after rain, so long
in the waiting, in the desert, waiting,

their blossoms so sudden, *ocotl*,
torches, burning. Whether their burning is the burning of
cities, the remembrance of Canyon de Chelly
when armies passed in the night to torch
houses, fields, and orchards
when the dogs and children died,

or whether it might be
my own heart, our hearts, inflamed

by some spark without reason—
the old hope and joy—
I cannot say.

THE DEAD of summer and nothing moves,
not the sky of weathered slate
nor the faces of strangers
pasted in their rooms above the street,
expressionless or strained. The joyous intervals
that pass us by are mute, committed now
to memory's coldest cells. *Once,*
the Poet sang, *once only.* And then
no more? The murky tide
that washed my feet draws slowly
back to sea. The young couple in the doorway
linger to embrace. This, and then the earth?

Yesterday was berries on the beach.
I dozed beside a fire and heard
or dreamed foghorns on a summer afternoon
like sirens enticing us
toward reefs
hidden by the waves. I woke then
chilly and afraid. The dead weight we carry
like an ancient grief is ours
because we will it—the lonely burden
of the verb *to be* as it becomes attached
to *living,* or *alive,* day by day. So it's not to say
we can't, or won't,
go on. But on this earth, in

the middle of our trespass, we are
invisible, we are only shadows
sliding into night, pausing to give names
to the things that shape our passing: *saguaro,*
thimble-berry, madrone. Or *charity.*
Or *love.* Tell me it isn't fruitless, this moment
in which Keith Jarrett breaks
my heart from a phonograph, or that moment
long ago when I was lost in

Beethoven's great pastoral as the wind
swept away the desert, endlessly.

So long as the tongue can
open to the vowel, so long as we can rise into
each day just once, rise, and rising,
move the hand
to *act*, it remains for us to praise:
the fine red dust that covers Escalante,
light rain or mist of summer
on the coast, almond groves
of the northern San Joaquin, the clarity
of temple bells, Kyoto
after rain. Could I feel
the fingers that brushed my lips
just once,
so very long ago, then
I could praise.

Goodbye, we say, meaning
happy passing,
or *kind beyond*. But we
are only shadows
pausing as we pass high over the earth to say
our little praise. The old madrone
that trembles in the wind
can't help us, the absolute calm of animal eyes at night
cannot be our calm. But once, once
leaning in a door
that opens the other world, we pass
our moment,
and suddenly know the earth
that we were a part of, once.

LOYALTY

FOR TREE AT THIRTY

after Akhmatova

THE HEART'S memory of sunlight grows dimmer
when the grass yellows.
The wind swirls up its few flakes
and even these are meager.

The thin canal lies still,
almost as if frozen over.
Nothing ever happens here
forever.

Against the smear of sky the willows
spread their bones like fans.
You're better off as you are:
never to be a wife.

If our memory of sunlight grows dimmer,
then what? The dark.
Okay. Then tonight we begin
the winter.

THE CARTOGRAPHER'S WEDDING

Nobody knows what love is anymore—
not the groom in his rental suit
flushed with desire, not the bride
blushing in her one-day dress and flowers
smouldering with the fires of expectation.
Nobody knows, and I least of all.

Still, we are here, against all reason,
the products of that ancient spoken
or unspoken vow. To the east, across
nearly insurmountable summits caked
with snow, the Great Plains rise
and fall while we continue to remain

steady as November rain, having grown
accustomed to a cold that never freezes,
to a shade of deep, spectacular green
intact, season after season. And so we find
ourselves outside in fog, in hoarfrost,
in rain or snow, living as we do

at the edge of a continent or a dream,
living perhaps with our hearts
not in our hands, but on our lips,
although they are seldom spoken.
(Friendship hereabouts is assumed
like an old mackinaw or a blanket.)

But that time comes, and it *will* come,
when you try to recite the names
or find the odd, almost familiar faces
that move beyond the old events, like fog,
that made you what you are. The years
that disappeared like falling stars

are lovely to remember. And there will
be time aplenty for flowers on a grave.
No, nobody knows what love is. Nobody
understands the past. Saddled with
all the hopes that will outlast
a lifetime's dedication, we,

groom, bride, friend and friend—
we step into the day amazed to find ourselves among companions eager to weather
the winds of change that turn us
heavenward, poor fools together,
never to learn what love is, we

who map the country where it lives.

ANYBODY'S GENIUS

WE WERE having dinner in a restaurant on the water
when a drunken sculptor joined us. He could have been
anybody's genius for all we knew. At least he kept us
entertained.
It has been years and years since we began
a life at war. As though through a Brechtian dream, the voice
says, "First the napalm, then the fall-out." And I turn
but no one's there. It has been ten years since you asked,
"What were they like?" and the silence answered back.

The days, the weeks and months roll by and the remembered
food
was great. And the wine was a language I cannot speak.
The sculptor's gone back to his island, and you
to the East.
It's no longer the simple question of stopping
a war before it's too late. It's already too late for that.
We join arms to form a picket line, but we laugh a lot.
Joy, too, is urgent, is also Fate and wants to ask,
"What are we like?" before the silence answers back.

HOMAGE TO TRAKL

The dead have their own tasks. —Rilke

1. De Profundis

BLACK RAIN in a stubbled field,
the lone brown tree, and a whisper
of wind to haunt the empty houses.

It is beautiful to walk
alone in the final silence of the light,
to gather the growing dark into
our arms as we go, to feel
its thistles.
               Far from the villages,
we can hear the insects call, the tides
riding the distances, and the evening animals
the mind supplies. I could tell you
how the skies turn to stars, how stars
first throb and then tremble, but you
have seen the night.
               I saw the good
light die upon your tongue and found
myself on a moor, lost among
rubble and waste and the strange
sounds that had no name,
                      stiff with cold,
terrified and beguiled by the song
dead angels sing to the wild. You are gone
into our blood, and dusty stars
tremble softly in the mire.

2. Helian

IN ITS LONELIEST hours, the spirit
loves a walk in the sun between
the yellow walls of summer.

Long evenings I wasted on wine,
chatter, the sweet sonata of laughter,
and the absolute stillness of night,—
these were the seeds of my planting.

I wandered the black labyrinth
of November and bowed my head
beneath decaying limbs where thrushes
sang alone in the darkness.

If I glimpsed the mad son, the deranged
sweat of his sleep, his weeping,—
no one ever saw him except it was night.

The dead are resurrected just at dusk
when a nameless goddess gapes, swallows light,
and slowly, slowly closes her deep blue eyes.

3. Lament at Grodek

TWIN EAGLES, Sleep and Death,
circle his head all night.
The icy wave of time lifts up
his bruise-blue body
and shatters it on the reef.

The sea sings its lament,
and the sisters of the sea
are quiet, the silent stars hesitate
and go out,
            the weapons fail.
Wrapped in the skirts of night,
his mouth broken, he bleeds
a long road leading into questions
only autumn answers.
                    Soon, he will
burst into flame, soon
his song will harden into bronze
and spill back over us
and hold us
and burn us black with shame.

4. To One Who Died Young

MY DARK ANGEL, my demented one,
you must have been a child
at one time, you must have descended
those stone steps in autumn in Mönchsberg
smiling strangely.
                          Could you hear
what the stones were singing, could you
smell the flesh that made the forest
green with hope and death,
                                could you hear
the deer's lament? What purple sun
died in the bare branches of the elm,
what flower turned to blood
as it blossomed on your tongue?

The evening bells were always blue
like this. The stars are always good.
You would have liked the stars tonight,
you would have walked alone and silent
under elms that line the riverbank.

LOYALTY: a letter

Concerning daily manual labor: Idleness is the enemy of the soul;
hence brethren ought at certain seasons to occupy themselves with
manual labor, and again at certain hours in holy reading.
                                                    —Cassiodorus

IT IS AUTUMN equinox again and the rain,
the rain is falling, as it did yesterday,
as it will tomorrow. I take up the pen
you found and wiped the mud from, and words
drip from my fingers
glistening on the page, this palimpsest
of my heart where I shall write out
the loyalties of a lifetime complete
with erasures and re-visions, mis-spelled
devotions across the sinuous
syntax of the years.
                        Pavese says
that if all men accepted work
there wouldn't be injustice in the world.
You who have gone down the road
in falling rain to dig a hole by hand
on your little plot of land—you know
and understand the simplicity of virtue,
the dignity of digging a shithouse hole
through how-many-feet of hardpan clay
in steady September rain. These ancient
convictions we hold in kind.
                            We are men
who love labor and women with whom
we can be friends. Our loyalties are few,
but thoroughly defined. I want to be
an old, beat-up guitar that sings
the blues—a siguriya—a canticle

for the damned. I want to be a comrade
to the soil. And when the days darken,
I will remember this pen you found,
remember the slate skies and the loyalty
of this land where words come as easily
as rain,
         where daily sweat and ordinary
tenderness accrue each day and are
the measure of the man. May we forget
the times we failed—but never
the reasons why. We revise our lives
to meet whatever consequence circumstance
demands. Low overhead, Ezra Pound reminds,
leaves room for a fuller life. Hip deep
in labor, give thanks to aching
arms and legs,
              coarse tongues to sing
of where you're from, where you're going,
to the stiff back that bends from time to time
in the basic gesture of religion: faith
in the common good. I want to be there
with you, to shape the lay of the land
into something fit for human habitation
where your neighbors can be coons, cranky
old coyotes, or common deer. These
are our teachers, the makers of devotion.

*   *   *

ALTHOUGH I come from the sudden
white-hot days of the desert, the sea
sings clearly in my ears, it is the sea
that rises through my blood: its tides
flood my eyes to shape and reshape
the continent of dreams. Exiled,
I no longer remember the yellow faces

of summer, rough-hewn hands smelling
of the stable. I stand alone awash with
nightfall, listening to the sea.

                                The wind-
stricken eaves groan against
the dark, and the sea is a grave
for friends who didn't make it, who died
of avarice, of greed. We owe them nothing
but the breathing alders do when no one
listens, when no one gambles it all
on the card of a single ambition. Like
a stone skipped into the waves. The wings
of night lift us up for our countrymen
to wound us, and

                        our little temporal
plot of ground we've heaped against the sea
can't hold us very much longer. Even soil
bleeds on the quick blades of lies. But
once, once when I touched someone—
a man, a woman, but someone I touched
with the thought of you—there came a
sudden touch in return that made me bend
to the earth again to lift a handful
to my lips:

                  it forgave us
everything. And so we must forgive
ourselves and our friends and the cock
that crows an hour before dawn, dis-
rupting our fragile dreams. This land
we bruise with malignant ambition
can never be our land. But we
belong to it. The sea may call us
into dream, the starlings set the fancy
into flight, the rains rinse us clean of
all our wounds and knives—

                             we remain

huddled against the earth while clouds
like waves wash up against the sky.
My friend, I offer this hand, knotted
in its pain, to hold your pick and shovel, to
dig a welcome burrow for your human
and therefore holy excrement. Though a man
is no better than a mole, he is nothing
without loyalty, without faith in labors,
without neighborly devotion.

THE ORACLE AT SUNRISE:
laborare est orare

THE TALL SHADOWS of nightfall climb back
toward the trees
as the first sun wavers through
the thick cream of fog.

As uncertain as the first promise
of morning, I fit the key to the lock, the doors
swing wide,
and I breathe in the scents of ink, typewash, and dry
alderwood stacked
beside the stove.

The dark banks of type
annoint me with their longing, their fitful
silent reminder
of saintly old masters: the Didots,
Bodoni, Claude Garamont,
Fournier, Morris and Morison,
Hermann Zapf, and funky Fred Goudy.

So cloistered
in this temple of ambition,
it is the hour
of black coffee and meditation, the hour of
breaking hearts through the mail and the kindling
of salvation. Some days
it is more than I can bear.

The old platen press—
no one
uses them anymore—hums
and chugs and clunks; the damp paper imported
from somewhere I've never been

blesses my fingers with
cool soft cotton kisses like
the whispers of the dead.

The little fire chuckles in the stove.
The old dog drowses
near the door. And although I know it
as hopeless, although heaven is the dream
of charlatans and fools, quaking in my fear,
I brace myself
to begin my morning prayer.

THE BODY OF SUMMER

THE JOURNEY

the heart/never fits/the journey
—Jack Gilbert

To BEGIN with, it begins
and ends with the heart, that long
tunnel with the darkness
at its end. So that the journey is a kind
of defeat the ordinary heart survives.

Like the man who buys flowers for his love—
of course, the flowers die. He dies.
Or she dies. Or is it their love.
Such a sequence of events we name The Journey
and which, that it might live, the heart contrives.

IN GEMINI

JUNE COMES over the hills to the plum trees
we planted in our yard this spring. Pruned down
and planted in sawdust and peat, their leaves
open in little clusters to the light
of heaven, to the light of summer's dawn.
The crows that gather in the alders there
grow boisterous, the robins search the ground
for tidbits, and the juncos swarm and trill.

How long this earth will last, I cannot say.
But I come again into the sunlit day
amazed, stunned by fields of green flame, flights
of youthful fancy I thought to leave behind.
Your hand in mine, we enter Gemini,
and little plum trees shower us with light.

THE BODY OF SUMMER

AFTER HOURS of small talk and music,
after the coffee and conversation,
I part your knees
to kiss you: your whole body buzzes
like a field of bees
and I savor the summer's honey.

THE BODY OF SUMMER

AT DAWN,
you wake me,
warm breasts pressed
against my thighs, your breath
warm and lingering.

Far to the south,
in forests dark with rain,
the temple bells are ringing.

CATULLI

MY WOMAN says she'd rather have me
than anyone; even if Jupiter proposed,
she says. But what an eager woman says to lovers
should be written out in winds and waters.

AFTER BILITIS

You CAME with heavy-lidded eyes,
your moist lips thirsting after mine,
and our tongues intertwined, searching.

My hands beneath your robe
felt you undulate, yield, turn,
stiffen, and suddenly shiver.

Your body pressed against me,
my knees were turned to water.
I love you like no other.

PASTORAL

CAN YOU STILL stand out on that balcony
and see far off across the tops
of stunted birch trembling in the winds
of spring, the dirty inlet piled high with snow
and ice, can you still hear
the drone of planes, the whine of single engines
curving over hills and houses
along the filthy streets? I see you
gazing through the long afternoon
at nothing,
waiting perhaps for some simple thing
that never comes, some gesture
from the land.

I remember the dark red wine
that nourished me like soil
when I explored the secret depths of tangled brush,
the soft blue pools of water,
the roses still hidden in their buds.
I, too, am hovering, a hummingbird,
a bee. Everything's like that—an old song
sung slightly out of key, a memory
of a gentle pastorale someone played once
perfectly. I, too, watch, but cannot see.
I listen for the land to have its say,
for the music of what may be.

VESPERS

HE STRETCHED out slowly in the grass
there on the hill above the river
where it enters the tides and the sea.
On his back, the sun warm and high,
he closed his eyes to listen:
from inside the little house, he heard
the gentle voices of women.

And he remembered once, a thousand
miles south on this same coast,
a different house, a different sun,
but the voices—even then they were warm.

SUMMER SOLSTICE, 40082

TRANSPARENT CLOUDS turn the sky pale blue.
It is the heart of the heart
of summer, and the longest day of the year.
The rhododendron flowers have all fallen,
but the garden is thick and new.
Tomorrow brings swallows and starlings,
tonight the moon will be clear.

A ROSE FOR SOLITUDE

A ROSE FOR SOLITUDE

I.

A MAN wades the deep north
bending into the day. Birch trees
are black against falling snow
whole mountains vanish in.
The flakes are wet and heavy
with spring. Already Cook Inlet
begins to break up, huge chunks
of ice thrust up, pools warmed
by last week's sun collecting
into currents. This sudden city
is gray against gray skies.

II.

THIS LIFE of ours, this fleeting moment
we are given—we enter it stunned
never to learn how
to perceive it. If we could only
touch the things of this world
at their center, if we could only hear
the tiny leaves of birch
struggling toward April,
then we could know.
                    But we walk on,
just as before, through deep snow,
through mile after mile
of deep snow, through mountains
and valleys of it, more snow
falling in huge wet flakes,
and never know just
how no two are alike.

III.
THE OLD poet
in his seventieth year
wrote, "Change rules
the world. / And man
but a little while." The moon
tonight will be full, it is
March of the year
forty-thousand eighty-two
on the secular calendar.
The old poet whom
I love is
dying. And I am suddenly in
the middle of my life.

IV.
IN THE FORTIETH dawn
of my journey, turning toward
my fortieth year, I turn
toward home. The path I follow
vanishes before my eyes.
When Su T'ung-po was
an old old man and lost his all,
when his house burned down, he laughed
and said, "Now I can see the stars!"

I who inhabit a fearful world
grow silent with the years. This world
is only process, a single
monumental motion
without beginning, without end. We like
to think this world is ours, but we
belong to it, to a world
just being born.

V.
THE CREAK of soft snow underfoot.
My breaths go out in little puffs
before me, only to disappear.
From far off I hear the rattle
and clatter of a train. No wind.
The ravens hop first
on this foot, then on that
around a scrap of bread.

For no reason, I suddenly feel
the small coal of my heart
suddenly flicker and grow.

VI.
THE MYSTICS say now that
the planets are aligning
there will be
a great change. Some
predict doom, some
predict glory. The planets
are nothing to me.
I say, It is snowing.

VII.
AND IF, as I pass, I look
into your eyes, do not be
afraid. I want to glimpse the void
at the center of your heart, I want
to reach out for you
because I know as you do that we
might never have met.

VIII.
"LIFE AFTER life after life
goes by," the poet said.
How many lives go by us in the day
never to touch this world?
How many bodies are shamed
by sudden light? Gray birds circle
and twine through the trees. They have
no cry. Each moment is
everything we have and more
than we can use.

IX.
THE FULL moon climbs
toward heaven. It lights
up the clouds with a light
like a pearl that is burning.
Darkness shuts out
the city like blowing
out a lamp. There is
nowhere to look
but up. All the graves
of the world are filled
with dead heroes, dead
lovers, and struggle.
So many lives
are graves. As the clouds
begin to move, the light
dies, is reborn, dies,
and grows again into
a long, slow, steady pulse
breathing through the night.

X.

YESTERDAY, in a colder climate,
alone in a frozen city,
a pilgrim climbed the streets
toward home. The wind
scorched his face, his
parka zipped tight, the hood
drawn close against chill.
Inside his shirt, clutched
against his heart, he held
a single long-stemmed rose.
The little bud was warmed
by whatever warmth he had.
It was a little flower
for nothing in this world.
Its thorns beaded his skin
with blood, the red bud
nestled against his nipple.
Somehow, in dead winter,
he carried it home to bloom.

XI.

Do NOT move.
Let the snow speak.
Let winter pass.
We ask
for truth
and the Year of the Dog
howls on.

XII.
THERE ARE others
wade the deep north.
Others will pass by
in reverence for
whatever this country knows.
Another may offer
a rose against
this solitude, a breath
for hope, a hand
to keep back the night.
Summer flies, and then
the snows return.
But we will never
be strangers again.

PERDIDA ETERNA

GEORGE SEFERIS IN SONORA

It is most true that eyes are form'd to serve
The inward light, . . .
  —Sydney, "Astrophel And Stella"

No, I CAN'T touch these mountains.
I have no word for the long shadows of saguaros
lengthened by the full moon of April. I've seen
how you wrap these mountains in highways, how
the natural numbers of Sonora accumulate
until you suddenly realize
they always total zero. At 4 a.m.
when the traffic dies and the moon embraces the Pacific,
I'm up
and drinking coffee, my nose in George Seferis.
Whatever you told me, I had to learn it by ear,
I had to memorize the touch—I couldn't believe my eyes.

How else to account for fingers that touched me once
and then vanished—of course they were roses
dying of the sun, they were songs doves sang
to begin another morning. It's always that
exactly: the untouchable other world
that touches us most deeply. Paris lay down
with a shadow, he lay down with an empty tunic,
and thousands died, but they didn't die
for Helen. It was no goddess or mortal
they died for: not Helen, but the idea of Helen betrayed them.
And surely this desert is a woman who knows

God first invented blood
and then the thirst for blood, that each man is a Paris
who returns, anonymous, clutching an empty tunic.
To speak of the desert I must return
to the Ancients, to the memory of some unspeakable failure.

Even to speak of Troy
in this city in Sonora, even to dream of Troy,—it is brutal.
So I rise, old somnophobiac, before the day begins,
to write in the blood of our race, to save
what cannot possibly be saved, and now
the first songbirds long before dawn, mockingbirds
add their *gloriae, gloriae* to the morning.

*   *   *

SOMETIMES the dove, that old cliché,
is more a moan than a song
when it sings *woe, woe*, and huddles on its limb.
A veil of fragile clouds
marbles the eastern sky. In Alexandria, they say,
it's the nightingale that wounds us. Here, we listen
to the terrible silence of the past, the enormous cost
of our decision to forget. Yesterday, as you trimmed
a dying bougainvillea, you pointed
across the way to another, entirely in blossom.
"They like the sun," you said, "and this one
gets very little." Oh, it was the color of blood,
it was beautiful all right.

And I wanted to give you a flower, but the garden
was all weeds, there were no roses, no asphodels
for me to bring to ease our mutual regret,
only these few coarse words
an old man sings in a broken voice when he's humbled
by a desert. There's a desert
each of us endures. It's beautiful there
and deadly. Whatever we give away
comes back to us, it's true, so I bring you
the whole of the moon as it passes, the fallen
petals of roses crushed into a powder,

this sort-of-a-song
that rattles my heart in its singing.

But it's not about a desert. No,
I can't reach your mountains, I have no word
for these highways wrapping a heart for storage.
When the moon returns
bulging with its promises and warnings,
I will have no word that can name them. The roads
that lead back from Sonora as though from the ancient temple
are a song a choir sings
in a long-forgotten language, the long body of our dreaming,
a lattice-work for rose-vines blooming by inward light
our eyes were made for seeing. And now,
in the harsh first light of day,
the mockingbirds sing *gloriae, gloriae absurdus*.

BETWEEN YOU AND ME

The lonely man—who's been in prison—goes back to prison
each time he eats a piece of bread.

—Cesare Pavese

EVERYWHERE there are walls.
But none so gray, none quite
so remoreslessly gray, as these.

You believe another life will come,
the smell of the saloon, the bite
wind takes coming over the tundra.

Each bitter cup of coffee steams
alone. Is it dark? Sunrise
is Memory's other name.

Still, there will be an evening
when your hands unravel the slow
secrets of a love, re-

learning that ancient form
of prayer. Behind you, the walls
will tremble with your shadows

till you glide through hazy air.
The bread you break, the soup
of hope, animals with nightfall

in their hair—these too
return in time. What the body
knows, it knows.

But the nouns, the nouns
grind down a man:
convict; prisoner; inmate.

I, too, am just a man.
I understand the dignity
of that. I never bought

those names for wrong
or right. I will curb
my taste, but

not my appetite.

IN THE COMPANY OF MEN

AT THE NORTHERN edge of this country
where the rain halts only
to be snow, the great glaciers wander
the slow indifferent centuries
toward the sea. Perched high
in frozen evergreens, real eagles
scan the bays below. No rag
wavering in the wind can set their hearts
to beat, no printed illustration
conveys the anger of their eyes,
nor the serious ease
only animals can attain. I walk
late morning sunrise near the bay.
The gray of dawn breaks over peaks
of gray as I listen to the gulls—
they bicker and squabble
over scraps thrown out from
wintered trawlers.
                   Yesterday,
having paid my final visit
to the inmates, Lemon Creek Prison,
the heavy doors banged finally closed
behind me, and I remembered again
the same doors from twenty-five
years before when I was still
a boy, and something sank
so far in me that I could not speak
its name. Not fear, but the leaden
hand of day-to-day despair
like a metal fist
clutching the heart
unmercifully. We, all of us,
are guilty. Yet the few endure

the great indignities
we all must share.
                    The scraps
I toss away are words, no more.
I want to offer hope, a hand
of brotherhood across the steely dark
to pay my share of the fee
for the pound of human flesh
that faceless angel of revenge demands.
I take away their faces carved
into my mind with razor blades: Allen,
who speaks Chinese and knows
the strength within; Tom's serious
eyes and undeveloped gift
for muscular description; Reggie,
who looked a thousand miles in me
the time I mentioned Malcolm.

Gray rain slanting narrow streets
can't blur the echo of strong voices.
The cold from which I shiver
is the cold of self, within. I walk alone
but am in the company of men,
and as I move a little closer to
the stone that marks what a life had been,
something in me cries, *Begin*.
Although I leave alone
as each of us
must do, we, all of us
together, are going slowly home.

A WORD FOR SPRING

We've returned; we always set out to return
to solitude, a fistful of earth, to the empty hands.
　　　　—Seferis, "A Word for Spring"

ONCE MORE we step
from the cold solitudes of winter
into the solitudes of spring. Once more
the yellow daffodils and lillies
are the cruellest month.
I used to love to walk down Water Street
where crates of oranges and bananas
and heads of cabbage and lettuce were
stacked shoulder-high. I used
to watch the unknown people pass
beside the miracle of the sea
talking to each other
as though the sea were a thousand
miles away and didn't know
the secrets of our blood.

Sometimes I think the sea is
listening to our lies, sometimes
I think it hears us groping in the dusk.
If it does, it remains
at ease despite us. If we could understand
the rhythms of the tides, if we
could reach into the shadows of the bay,
we too could sleep through the long
and lengthening sunshine of
the day. Instead, we pause
between the coffee and the cigarette,
between the talk that wakes us and the sleep
of solitude that punctuates

our speech, studying our hands
like exiles bent above a map
that set us on our way.

The secret meeting place
where water and land join hands
could be our place. Were it not
for the red and white of our veins,
our hearts would pump pure
sea water to our minds and lungs
and we would learn to breathe
according to the moon. But we
are lonelier than that. Someday soon
the old days will come back. I loved
the bread I broke between my hands, the taste
of wine from someone's lips, the emptiness
of Water Street at night when spring
was ripe and everything was mine.

KAH TAI PURGATORIO

I COULD carry a little boat out
through sandy hillocks and marsh grass
and slip it into the water and slide
over that blue-green glass in silence.

I could cruise the water-course of winds
around this small lagoon where
terns nestle into shadows and herons wade.
I could, I could.

I want, like this little body of water,
to let my body reflect the stars and moons
of midnight. I want to lie that still.
I've seen this water calm as a dreamy boy.

But then I'd have to, sooner or later,
return. And doing so, I'd have to choose,
and any bank I chose
would be the world.

TO A BLUE HERON

I WISH I could have made that place
for you—down there
among the marsh grass and purple-blooming thistle
and scotchbroom where everyone
dumps beer cans and broken toys and whatever
is passing from their lives. Now
you and I have passed.

I might have been drunk or hung over,
but hurting at any rate
when I pulled over and stopped
the truck to walk out into the moonlight
in the fog, shivering
with some cold
more internal than the weather.

I would gladly
have been a woman for you
if you could have been a man. I would
have gathered you into my arms and held
you tight against my breast
like a dying child for want
of another life. But you were still
in the night, and far away.

Off on a hill above the fog,
a nighthawk beeped. Below, a few tall spruce
combed out the hair of mist.
I didn't know what I wanted,
though I knew I would die
for the asking. And you, too, are
dying, but you have more grace
than to sing it.

All it will take is one old man
fishing alone in the water, one woman
rocking alone in the dark, a moment
of silence like a monument in the middle of
the day, and we will be forgotten.
I wouldn't change that
for a thing.

NIHIL OBSTAT

THE BEES are building stairways toward heaven.
Soon the world will cloud over and the bees
will fall silent and die among the dead blossoms
of scotchbroom and thistle.
                                        We who often buzz
among our own works will not listen. This
is called natural history and is left
for specialists to explain. Someday everything
will be explained in the footnotes of basalt
and granite, in igneous thumbprints
of another century.
                                        For now, there is the song
September sings to welcome home the autumn.
We cannot save the bees. We cannot save
each other.
                        The birds of prey that stagger
down the skies will wait for us
at the other end of history,
                                        as we, stung
by the brevity of our song, enter
the resonant long corridor of dying light
that leads us not toward heaven,
                                        but toward home.

HELENIC TRIPTYCH

FOREHEAD on forearms, eyes unfocused,
he listens to rain pelting wet earth that smells
of dreams and destinations, of departures that preceded
no arrivals. Alone with the long afternoon,
he longed for starlight through windows,
for the soft hollow breath of the sea as it sounds
through the broken conch of the human voice
traveling its distance alone.

There was a time he thought of his body
as a temple for Helen, a time when the twin fires of his tongue
were his daughters, Justice and Mercy, but
that is the way of the young. Helen,
kidnapped by Theseus much as our bodies are taken:
for the moment—before the life escapes into Hades—
and we waken to dawn confused, everything forgotten,
everything but Helen.

And so he sets sail from Troy, forehead
bent to forearm, the afternoon slipping by
with its cargo of dream and remembrance.
So that is how the summer died.

*   *   *

At dawn, he'd taken
a solitary step and entered
the nearly perfect syntax of the world.

It would be simple to die for Helen.
It would be easy to set sail, to turn one's back on the ruins,
to acquire the grammar of wisdom

at the small cost of some small life:
to construct a civilization.

Arrival is not destination, nor death
a suitable answer.

Each step the first step, each step the final:
each road a crossroad: each tree
articulates a tree: it is that which comes closest
but passes, that suggestion of perfection,
that makes the flesh its home.

*   *   *

And now, he knows, the evening comes
with its torment and its thugs
demanding taxes. And then the anonymous night
with its quicklime of desire,
its starlight and retribution.

That is how this window came to look out
on grief, on the charred monuments of Troy:
it would be good to give one's life for the beautiful
if the beautiful would last. But the world
casts us out and it is impossible to touch anything
except one another. So we reach out when we can

for the out-stretched hand of another
knowing that when it is withdrawn . . .

Head tilted foreward
almost as though to pray, he buries
his eyes in his forearm.
And the gesture is almost perfect.